Beast Quest ®

Collect the special coins in this book.
You will earn one gold coin for
every chapter you read.

Once you have finished all the chapters,
find out what to do with your gold coins at
the back of the book.

With special thanks to Cherith Baldry

For Rachel Leyshon

www.beastquest.co.uk

ORCHARD BOOKS
Carmelite House
50 Victoria Embankment
London EC4Y 0DZ

A Paperback Original
First published in Great Britain in 2008
This edition published in 2015

Beast Quest is a registered trademark of Beast Quest Limited
Series created by Beast Quest Limited, London

Text © Beast Quest Limited 2008
Cover illustration © David Wyatt 2008
Inside illustrations by Steve Sims © Beast Quest Limited 2008

A CIP catalogue record for this book is available from
the British Library.

ISBN 978 1 40834 769 0

1 3 5 7 9 10 8 6 4 2

Printed in Great Britain by Clays Ltd, Elcograf S.p.A.

Orchard Books
An imprint of Hachette Children's Group
Part of The Watts Publishing Group Limited
An Hachette UK Company

www.hachette.co.uk

Beast Quest®

Zepha
THE MONSTER
SQUID

BY ADAM BLADE

ORCHARD

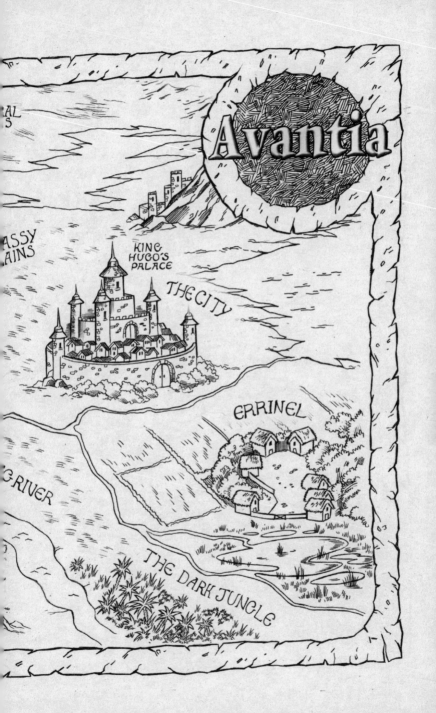

CONTENTS

Did you think it was over?

Did you think I would accept defeat, and disappear?

No! That can never be. I am Malvel, the Dark Wizard who strikes fear into the hearts of the people of Avantia. I still have much more to show this kingdom, and one boy in particular...Tom.

The young hero liberated the six Beasts of Avantia from my curse. But his fight is far from over. Let us see how he fares with a new Quest, one that will surely crush him and his companion, Elenna.

Avantia's Beasts had good hearts that I corrupted for my own wicked purpose. Now, thanks to Tom, they are free to protect the kingdom once more. But now I bring to Avantia six Beasts whose hearts are evil and so cannot be set free: monster squid, giant monkey, stone charmer, snake man, king of spiders and three-headed lion. Each one guards a piece of the most precious relic of Avantia, which I have stolen: the suit of Golden Armour that gives magical strengths to its rightful owner. I will stop at nothing to prevent Tom collecting the complete suit and defeating me again. This time he will not win!

Malvel

PROLOGUE

King Hugo's master of arms paused at the foot of the stairs. He smiled to hear the faint noise of music and laughter from the Great Hall above.

Thank goodness, he thought. *Malvel the Dark Wizard has been defeated. Avantia is safe again.*

He walked down the stone passage and stopped outside a heavy padded door, studded with brass nails. He pulled a slender golden key from his pocket and held it up. It shone in a ray of light that reached down from an air vent and pierced the gloom of the palace cellars.

The key turned smoothly when he fitted it into the lock. He pushed the door open and stepped into the arms room, closing the door behind him and locking it. As he did so, a ferret poked its head out of his pocket and peered up at him with bright, curious eyes.

"There we are," the master of arms murmured, stroking the ferret's cream-coloured fur. "Now no one can get in or out."

The room was so small that if the man stretched out his arms, his fingers brushed the walls on either side. Torches blazed in iron holders, casting dancing shadows on the rough stone walls.

In the centre of the room stood a golden suit of armour on a wooden stand. The helmet was dramatically moulded into the shape of an eagle's head; the visor was a sharp beak and the rest of the helmet was engraved with feather-like patterns. The golden chainmail vest was covered with a fine breastplate that shone in the torchlight. Glittering leg armour, gauntlets and sabatons – armoured boots – completed the suit.

The master walked slowly around it, examining the armour with a small grunt of satisfaction. He pulled out a handkerchief to rub a speck of dust from the gleaming breastplate.

"I've looked after this armour for twenty years," he said. "When I first set eyes on it, it took my breath away. And do you know what?" He tickled the ferret's ear. "It still does."

The ferret let out a squeak.

"It's the most precious relic in all Avantia. We've got to keep every bit of it shining as brightly as the day it was made," he went on. "Its rightful owner could return at any moment." He passed the handkerchief over the smooth curve of the helmet. "We must be ready." He bent down to polish the golden boots of the armour.

Suddenly the ferret let out a squeal of alarm. Wriggling out of its master's pocket, it dived for a crack in the wall and disappeared.

"Here!" the man cried. "What's the matter with you?" He put his head on the floor and tried to peer into the crack, but the dancing shadows cast by the torches made it difficult to see. "Where are you? Come back, you silly creature! There's nothing to be afraid of."

But as he spoke, the shadows began to leap, faster and faster, and were soon whirling across the walls and floor. He glanced at the torches, but the bright flames burnt steadily. What could be making the shadows swoop like this?

Then something brushed the man's cheek. He spun round at the velvety touch and stared wildly around the room. "These aren't shadows," he said out loud. "They're bats!"

Suddenly the air was full of black wings. Tiny claws scratched at his face and hands, and tangled in his hair.

"No!" He let out a choking cry and beat desperately at the air, trying to drive the creatures back. But the swarming bats kept coming. He stared in horror at their fierce faces and sharp teeth. Their little eyes glittered cruelly.

Terrified, the master of arms backed towards the door, as more bats squeezed themselves out of cracks in the wall and launched themselves into the air. He felt as if he couldn't breathe.

Soon the suit of armour was covered with bats. They hung all over it, clinging with their hooked claws. Gasping in horror, the master of arms started forward, but his knees gave way and he collapsed to the floor. Still he kept on struggling, trying with all his might to drag himself towards the precious armour.

"Stop!" he gasped. "Help! Please, somebody, help!"

But it was too late. Bats covered the man's head and back, wrenching his hair and suffocating him with their wings. He felt as if every last scrap of air was being pressed out of his lungs, and stared in disbelief as the Golden Armour rose slowly into the air, lifted by the evil swarm of bats. Only the wooden stand was left. Then darkness flooded over him.

GONE!

Tom stood next to a pillar in the Great Hall of King Hugo's palace, and watched the dancing. He was elated to see all the king's subjects celebrating the end of his Quest. Their silk and satin robes shone as they whirled in the afternoon sun.

King Hugo watched from the High Table with a contented smile. Tom knew the king was happy that the six Beasts of Avantia had been released from the evil spell of the Dark Wizard, Malvel. Ferno the Fire Dragon, Sepron the Sea Serpent, Arcta the Mountain Giant, Tagus the Horse-man, Nanook the Snow Monster and Epos the Flame Bird were now protecting Avantia instead of destroying it. The kingdom could begin to recover.

But Tom couldn't join in the celebrations. Something had been nagging at him ever since that final meeting with Malvel on the mountainside in the far east of the kingdom. He told himself over and over again that Malvel had fallen into the volcano and perished in its raging fires.

But he couldn't forget what Malvel had screamed at him just before he disappeared: "This is not the end, Tom! We shall meet again!"

Tom had a horrible feeling that he hadn't seen the last of his enemy. Then he remembered the hooded figure he had spotted in the cheering crowd when he returned from freeing Epos, the last of the cursed Beasts. If the Dark Wizard had indeed survived, how would he take revenge for his defeat?

Tom shuddered. He wished his father, Taladon the Swift, were here. He had been a knight and had undertaken a Beast Quest of his own. Only he could know how Tom felt. But no one had seen Taladon for many years. It was as if he had disappeared into thin air, although Tom felt certain that they would meet again one day.

Tom felt a hand on his shoulder. He turned to see Elenna, the friend who had shared every step of the Quest with him. She was wearing a dress of blue silk, but her short dark hair stuck out untidily, just as when they'd first met.

"What's the matter, Tom?" she asked. "Why are you looking so worried?"

Tom shook his head uneasily. "I'm not sure... I just keep remembering the last thing that Malvel said on the mountain."

"Malvel is finished," Elenna

declared. "There's nothing to worry about." Taking Tom's hand, she dragged him onto the dance floor. "I've just been to the stables. Storm is stuffing himself with the best apples, and look – Silver's enjoying himself under the table there."

Tom smiled as he saw the wolf contentedly gnawing on a bone, and was glad to think of his black stallion enjoying a well-deserved rest in the comfortable palace stables.

"Everyone's happy," Elenna went on. "Can't you be happy, too? Let's dance."

"I don't know how to dance," Tom said, laughing despite his worries.

"I'll show you."

To Tom's relief, the music stopped before Elenna could guide him through more than a few steps.

Then he spotted King Hugo's most trusted adviser, Aduro, making his way towards them. They would never have completed the Quest if it hadn't been for the Good Wizard, who had helped and encouraged them in their most difficult moments. Now he wore a magnificent embroidered robe and carried a polished wooden staff in one hand.

"Are you enjoying yourselves?"
Aduro asked.

"Yes, it's wonderful!" Elenna's eyes
sparkled.

The wizard smiled. "If you don't
mind missing some of the dancing,
I've something to show you.
Something in the palace cellars."

"Not more danger?" Tom was
instantly alert.

Aduro shook his head, smiling
again, and Tom realised that even
the king's adviser thought Malvel
had been defeated for good. "No," the
wizard replied. "It's a reward for a
successful Quest. Avantia owes you a
great deal."

Tom and Elenna followed him
to a small door at the far end of

the hall and down a long flight of steps. Elenna was bouncing with excitement.

At the foot of the steps was a narrow passage. Aduro led them on, then stopped outside a padded door. A single shaft of light shone down from a high air vent and gleamed on the door's brass nails and lock.

"This is strange," the wizard said. "I was expecting to meet the king's master of arms here. He's not the sort of man to be late. I wonder what has happened to him?"

"Maybe he's inside," Elenna suggested.

Aduro turned the door handle, but the door remained shut. "Locked," he muttered. "Maybe—"

He broke off at the sound of a loud groan coming from inside the room. Tom and Elenna exchanged a glance.

"It sounds as if someone's hurt," said Tom.

Wizard Aduro laid the end of his staff against the lock and commanded, "Open!"

The lock clicked and the door swung open. Inside the room the body of an elderly man sprawled on the floor. A ferret was nosing anxiously at him. The man tried to get up, but his strength gave way and he slumped down again.

Tom and Elenna ran to his side. He was barely conscious. His skin was pale, his black tunic was torn, and his face and hands were covered

with tiny bites and scratches.

Tom helped the old man to sit up.

"Aduro, can you magic a jug
of water for him?" Elenna asked.
"Quickly!"

But the wizard simply stared at
the space in the middle of the room,
empty except for a wooden armour
stand. He didn't seem to have heard

Elenna's anxious plea. He looked stunned.

Tom jumped to his feet. "What's the matter?" he asked.

Aduro turned to him, blinking as if he were just waking up. "Something terrible has happened." His voice was hoarse. "The Golden Armour. It's gone!"

2

A NEW QUEST

"Can you tell us what happened?"
Aduro asked, kneeling beside the
injured man.

The master of arms drew in a
shaky breath. "Bats!" he whispered.
"The whole room was full of bats.
They took the armour." He covered
his face with his hands. "I have failed
the king."

Aduro touched the old man's

shoulder. "No, my friend. Evil has been at work here." Standing up again, he thumped on the floor three times with his staff.

A moment later, Tom heard running footsteps in the passage and two servants appeared in the doorway. Their eyes grew wide with shock as they looked inside.

"Carry the master to his room,"
Wizard Aduro ordered. "Send for
King Hugo's healer. And mind you
say nothing of this to anyone."

The two servants lifted the elderly
man carefully. Elenna scooped up the
ferret and gave it to the master as he
was carried out into the passage.

As soon as the master of arms and
the servants had gone, Tom turned to
the wizard. "This was Malvel's work!
It must have been. He is still alive
after all."

Aduro nodded gravely. "I fear you
are right."

"What armour were you talking
about?" Elenna asked. "Why is it so
important?"

"Tom, the armour was to have been

your reward, for completing the Quest," Aduro explained. "Once it belonged to the Master of the Beasts. It brings magical strengths to its rightful owner."

"But..." Tom was puzzled. "You couldn't give me the armour if it belongs to the Master of the Beasts. I remember you told me that Malvel had imprisoned him long before my Quest began, but why isn't he still wearing it?"

Aduro let out a long sigh. "Some time ago, the Master of the Beasts should have returned to the palace for the New Year feast. Instead, the empty suit of armour appeared in the Great Hall as the nobles were taking their places." The wizard paused, then went on. "Malvel had captured him, then sent the armour to mock King Hugo – and me."

Tom felt as if an icy hand had clutched his heart. He hoped that the Master of the Beasts had not suffered too greatly in the hands of the Dark Wizard.

"However, I felt that all was not lost," Aduro said. "The powers of the armour would still work if the suit was worn by the right person – a true Quester with brave blood running through his veins. I think you are that person, Tom."

For a moment Tom couldn't speak. He wasn't sure he was worthy to wear the armour. But he would give everything to protect Avantia.

The wizard began to pace back and forth impatiently across the small room, his staff clicking on the stone floor. "Malvel must have realised that your successful Quest has made you a danger to him. He would never have imagined that anyone – much less a boy – could lift the spells on all six Beasts. He has stolen the armour to stop you wearing it and gaining its magical powers."

"But it would never fit me." Tom measured himself against the wooden stand that had held the armour. "It must have been made for a tall man."

"The armour will shrink or expand to fit the one who wears it," Aduro explained. "It will know who truly deserves it."

"Then we have to do something!" Elenna's eyes sparkled with indignation. "We can't let Malvel get away with this."

More cautiously, Tom added, "But first we must find out what really happened to the armour."

Aduro halted in his pacing. He raised his staff and swept it in a wide arc. The air glittered in its wake and a picture gradually formed, hovering above them.

Tom and Elenna let out gasps of wonder and fear.

They could see a multitude of flying bats, carrying pieces of the Golden Armour hooked in their claws. Then the swarm split up.

Groups of bats flew off in six different directions, each carrying a part of the armour. The sound of Malvel's mocking laughter grew until it filled the room.

The vision faded. When it had quite gone, Aduro let out a weary sigh. "This is worse than I feared. Malvel's bats have scattered the armour around the kingdom." He looked gravely at Tom. "Are you ready for another Quest, so soon after your

first? Will you seek out the pieces
of armour and bring them back
together?"

Tom drew himself up. "Of course I
will."

"And what about me?" Elenna
asked with a fierce look. "Where
Tom goes, I go!"

A relieved smile spread over
Aduro's face. "Thank you, Elenna. I
know that you too have the courage
to succeed. My magic map will show
you where to go. I'll fetch it while
you change into travelling clothes.
Meet me in the stables as soon as
you can."

Tom hurried back to his room
and changed into a woollen tunic
and sturdy boots. He fastened on

his scabbard, sheathed his sword and picked up his shield. It bore the six magical tokens from the Beasts he had freed: Ferno's dragonscale protected him from heat, Sepron's tooth from onrushing water, Arcta's eagle feather from great heights, and Nanook's bell from extreme cold. Tagus's horseshoe fragment gave him extra speed and Epos's golden talon healed wounds.

Surely their combined power would strengthen him now?

Then Tom went down to the stables. As he crossed the courtyard Elenna caught up with him, Silver at her heels.

"I took some food left over from the feast," she said, showing Tom a large bundle wrapped in a cloth.

"Good thinking,"Tom said, smiling. He knew he and Elenna made a great team.

Aduro was waiting in the stables. A groom had already saddled Storm. Elenna stroked the black stallion's nose and fed him one last apple.

"Here is the magic map."The wizard held the familiar parchment scroll out to Tom. "Guard it well. And take care. This time Malvel knows you are a threat to him. His magic is clearly as strong as ever, and now he is angry."

"I'm not afraid of Malvel,"Tom said bravely, resting his hand on the hilt of his sword.

Storm snorted, rapping one hoof

against the stable floor, and Silver let out a howl of agreement.

Tom climbed into Storm's saddle and Elenna scrambled up behind him.

"Farewell," said Aduro. "And may good luck go with you."

He ordered the guards to open the gates of the palace.

Tom urged Storm into a trot. As they passed through the gates, with Silver bounding alongside, Tom could still hear music and the sounds of celebration ringing out from the palace walls. The rest of Avantia had no idea that Malvel was alive and plotting once more.

Tom was determined that the Dark Wizard would not succeed. He and

Elenna would follow this new Quest to the end.

I'm ready, Tom thought. *While there's blood in my veins, I'll do everything I can to protect my home!*

MALVEL'S WARNING

"I'm glad you're here," Tom told Elenna as they rode away from the palace. "I know we can do this together."

"Silver and Storm will help us, too," Elenna said. "And don't forget the Beasts. They're friendly now, and it's their job to protect Avantia. Maybe we can call on them to help us fight Malvel."

"That's true," said Tom, feeling a swell of determination. With Elenna, their animal friends and the Beasts of Avantia on his side, he knew that it was his destiny to defeat the Dark Wizard.

The road they were following led through fields where cattle grazed peacefully. A few trees grew here and there in the lush grass; the afternoon sun cast long shadows.

Soon they came to a crossroads. Tom brought Storm to a halt and pulled out Wizard Aduro's enchanted map. As he unrolled it a red path began to glow, leading to the coast.

"That's the road we took when

we met Sepron the Sea Serpent,"
Elenna pointed out, peering over
Tom's shoulder.

"Then at least we know the way."
Tom felt more cheerful. He rolled
up the map, put it back in the
saddlebag, and urged Storm on.

They passed through a narrow
belt of trees and began to climb a
hill. Tom noticed that the sunlight
was growing hazy, as though night
was falling. A chill wind whispered
over him. But the sun still stood well
above the horizon, and the sky was
blue except for a few puffs of white
cloud. Uneasily Tom glanced around.
He couldn't see anything except
trees and fields.

Then he looked up. High above

in the blue sky, black dots were flitting back and forth. Tom remembered the vision Aduro had shown them. "Bats!" he exclaimed.

He felt Elenna lock her arms tightly around his waist. "I thought bats only flew by night," she said.

"Malvel can make his bats fly anytime," Tom replied grimly.

He reined Storm in, and gripped the hilt of his sword, ready to draw it. The black stallion threw his head up and his harness jingled. Beside the horse, Silver stood stiff-legged, barking angrily at the sky.

The bats flew lower and lower, until they were swooping around Tom and Elenna. Storm snorted nervously; Tom patted his neck to

reassure him. Silver leapt into the
air, snapping vainly at the leathery
wings.

Tom and Elenna had to duck to
avoid the creatures' talons. Tom
didn't dare try to outrun them on

Storm – the path was steep and rough, and the stallion could easily have been injured. Desperately he drew his sword and slashed at the whirling pack of bats. They fluttered upwards out of range and then clustered together in a rolling ball.

Elenna gasped in astonishment. "What are they doing?"

Slowly the ball took on a different shape. Icy fear rushed through Tom as he recognised the hooded being that had laughed at him so cruelly on that mountainside. It stretched across half the sky, from above Tom's head to the distant horizon.

"Malvel!" he exclaimed.

The Dark Wizard was using the
bats to give form to his evil face.
Tom could see the gleam of his
sunken eyes and the twisted line of
his cruel mouth. Mocking laughter
poured out and Malvel's voice

boomed around them.

"I hope you enjoyed my surprise. Fools, to think you can defeat me!"

Tom raised his sword. "I know we can defeat you. We'll track down every piece of the armour that you have stolen. Nothing is going to stop us!"

Malvel's laughter echoed again. "Nothing? Not even six new Beasts with evil hearts?"

For a moment Tom was shocked into silence.

Silver let out a miserable whine, and hurled himself into the air again, snapping at Malvel's shape.

"Evil Beasts!" Elenna exclaimed. "What does he mean?"

Malvel replied. "You'll find out

soon enough, when you meet Zepha. Maybe then you'll change your minds and go running home with your tails between your legs."

"Never!" Tom cried defiantly. "You can bring whatever Beasts you like, but they won't stop me. I'll never fail Avantia!"

But who – or what – was Zepha? Tom felt a lurch of fear in the pit of his stomach as he thought of the six evil Beasts he would have to face.

Then the bats began to scatter. Malvel's face broke up and disappeared, but his jeering laughter echoed around the hills until every last bat had vanished.

Tom sheathed his sword. His

stomach was still churning. Elenna looked white and shaken. Storm was sweating and trembling, and Silver's tail was dragging in the dust of the road.

"I think we should make camp," Tom said, trying to keep his voice firm. "We need time to get over that. And the sun's going down. It'll be dark soon."

Elenna nodded in agreement. They dismounted and Tom led the way to a small clump of woodland not far from the road. There was a pool in the middle of the trees, at the bottom of a rocky hollow. Tom unsaddled Storm while Elenna collected wood and made a fire. They were both glad of the bright

flames as the sun set and darkness
crept around them.

Elenna unpacked the food
she had saved from the feast
and handed Tom some bread
and cold chicken. "I wonder
why Aduro didn't warn us about

the evil Beasts," she said.

"Perhaps he doesn't know about them," Tom replied. "This is a different Quest. We can't rely on Aduro for everything. This time we're on our own."

Elenna's eyes shone with determination. "We'll manage," she said. "We've got to."

When they had finished eating Tom lay down beside the remains of the fire. He gazed up into the sky. The moon was sailing behind wisps of cloud; there was no sign of any bats.

But now Tom knew that something else was out there. Something more dangerous than Malvel's vicious bats.

Another set of evil Beasts.

Maybe they were already padding around him, hidden by the night. Tom peered into the shadows, but he couldn't see anything.

It took a long time for sleep to come.

DANGER AT SEA

By noon the next day they were near the coast. Tom remembered how they had struggled through the flood waters that Sepron the Sea Serpent had caused in his rage. Now the land was clear again, with crops growing and people working in the fields, and the houses had been repaired with new wood and thatch. Tom felt proud that he had helped make Avantia prosperous again.

At last the road led Tom and his friends through a patch of thin woodland and out onto the shore.

"Look!" exclaimed Elenna, pointing. "All the fishermen's huts have been rebuilt. And there are lots of new fishing boats."

At first Tom was pleased to see the snug new huts and the brightly painted boats pulled up on the beach, with fishing nets piled high beside them. Then he frowned.

"Shouldn't all those boats be out at sea?" he asked. He exchanged an uncertain glance with Elenna. "What's going on here?"

"There's a smell of dead fish, too," said Elenna, wrinkling her nose.

Tom spotted a wisp of smoke rising from behind some boulders further along the beach. He and Elenna dismounted. Leaving Storm to crop the grass under the trees, they headed for the rocks. As they drew closer they saw a group of people crouched around a driftwood fire. One woman was ladling stew from an iron pot into wooden bowls. All the people looked worried and miserable.

Then Tom recognised a boy with red hair and a freckled face. "Callum!" he exclaimed.

The boy looked up, and sprang to his feet. "Tom!" He hugged Tom and then Elenna, before bending down to plunge his hands into the thick fur round Silver's neck. "It's good to see you again."

"It's good to see you, too," Tom said. He would never forget how Callum had helped him when he came to free Sepron the Sea Serpent from Malvel's evil spell.

"What's going on here?" Elenna asked.

"Yes, why is no one out in the boats?" Tom added.

The men and women round the fire exchanged nervous glances.

"It's too dangerous to go out to sea," Callum explained after a moment's hesitation. "A couple of our people didn't come back yesterday. We found wreckage washed up, but no one knows what happened to the boatmen."

Tom glanced swiftly at Elenna. She was looking as confused as he felt. Sepron was free now, and should have been protecting this part of the kingdom. What had gone wrong?

"Do you know why they disappeared?" he asked Callum.

A man Tom recognised as Callum's father pointed out to sea.

"Whirlpools," he said. "They appeared a few days ago near those rocks. No one knows why. Only a fool would go out there now."

"Or Lindon," another man said with a bitter laugh.

"Who's Lindon?" Tom asked.

"A stubborn fool," the man replied. "He doesn't know what's good for him," a woman chimed in. "He insisted on going out this morning, trawling for fish, just as he always does. He hasn't returned yet."

"And goodness knows why he went," Callum's father added grumpily. "The pickings are thin enough. Since the whirlpools appeared, all the fish have gone."

"Some of them have been washed up dead," Callum said, pointing to the edge of the water.

Tom could see the gleam of silver fish lying among the other debris. Silver trotted down to the water's edge and snuffled at one of them. Then he drew back with a disgusted snort.

"Silver! Here, boy." Elenna tickled

the wolf's ears as he returned to her. "Be careful where you push your nose."

"These were good fishing waters," the woman went on. "But if the whirlpools stay, we'll have nothing but a few vegetables to live on."

Tom gazed at Callum. The boy's eyes were filled with hope. He was the only one from this village who

knew that Tom had freed Sepron
from Malvel's curse.

"I think I might know something
about this," Tom said softly, so that
only Callum could hear. "Wait here."

Beckoning to Elenna, he hurried
back to where they had left Storm.
He pulled the magic map out of
the saddlebag. When he unrolled it,
he could see a picture of a golden
helmet resting in the sea beside a
rocky islet.

"That's exactly where the
whirlpools are," said Elenna.

Tom met her anxious gaze. His
pulse began to race with a mixture
of fear and excitement.

"You heard what Callum said,"
Elenna went on. "Boats that go out

there don't come back."

Tom gazed out across the waves. "We don't have a choice," he said. "This is our Quest. We have to go."

1

5

LINDON

Tom put the map back into Storm's saddlebag. As he turned to the shore once again, he spotted a fishing boat sailing round a headland towards the beach, its white sail billowing.

"That must be Lindon," he said. "Maybe he'll take us out to the whirlpools in his boat. Come on!"

Tom and Elenna hurried down to the water's edge, Silver and

Storm trotting behind.

The boat soon reached the beach, and the fisherman leapt out and pulled it up beside the other vessels. He lifted the reed baskets out of the boat, but Tom could see there were only a few fish at the bottom.

"Are you Lindon?" Tom asked.

"That's me." The fisherman dumped the last basket on the beach and

straightened up. He was a tall young man with shaggy dark hair. His face was harsh and unfriendly. "Who wants to know?"

"I do. I need to go out to sea. Will you take me?"

"I might, if the price is right," Lindon replied. "Where do you want to go?"

"Over there." Tom pointed out

towards the rocky islet.

Lindon raised his eyebrows. "There are whirlpools out there. That will cost extra."

Tom exchanged a glance with Elenna. "I can't afford to pay you," he began, "but—"

"That's all right." Tom realised that Lindon was staring past him at Silver. "You can pay in kind. I'll take that mutt off your hands."

Elenna stepped in front of the wolf. She looked furious at the suggestion that she would hand over her faithful friend. The hair on Silver's spine rose up and he let out a soft growl.

"We can't do that," Tom said firmly. "Isn't there something else you want? Or anything we could do for you?"

Lindon narrowed his eyes. "Why do you want to go out there, anyway?" he asked.

Tom knew he couldn't tell anyone about his Quest. The first time had been bad enough, with the Good Beasts of Avantia under terrible curses. But now that Malvel had unleashed his own evil creatures on the kingdom it was even more vital to keep the Quest a secret. The people of Avantia would panic if they knew what the Dark Wizard was up to.

"I have something important to do," he said.

Lindon let out a bark of rough laughter. "Something important? A boy like you? You'll have to tell me more than that if you want my help."

Tom saw that Elenna was red with anger on his behalf. He had to act quickly before she said something they would both regret.

He remembered then how the people of the village had suggested Lindon liked to take risks. Maybe he would help if he thought that Tom was looking for danger.

"I want to see if I can survive diving into a whirlpool," Tom said, puffing out his chest. "And I've also heard all your fish have died. Maybe I can discover what's causing it."

Lindon stared at him for a moment in astonishment. Then he laughed. "Well, you're a mad one and no mistake," he said and paused, a sly look passing over his face. "If you don't come back, I'll have your fine-looking horse." He nodded to Storm, who pawed the ground. "If you do make it, I'll just shake you by the hand and wish you well." He sighed. "Who knows? Maybe you can find out what's killing our fish. We'll all starve if it continues."

Tom stroked Storm's neck. "Don't worry, boy, I'll be back," he said reassuringly, but he couldn't ignore the swelling fear in his stomach.

Tom had faced danger before. But now he had to defeat Zepha and find the golden helmet. Because if he didn't he would lose his horse, if not his life– and the Golden Armour would remain in Malvel's clutches.

OUT TO SEA

"I'm coming with you," Elenna said, as Lindon made the boat ready.

"No," Tom told her. "Defeating Zepha and finding the helmet is my task. I need you to stay here and look after Silver and Storm."

Elenna bit her lip, then nodded. Tom unfastened his scabbard and handed it to her.

"You might need this," he said.

"And my shield is tied to Storm's saddle. The people here are desperate; they could be dangerous. And you never know what Malvel might do."

Elenna hesitated. "But won't you need your sword and shield?" she asked.

Tom knew he would be vulnerable without them – but there was no way he was leaving Elenna alone and unarmed. He'd just have to rely on his wits. He took Elenna's hand and wrapped her fingers round the hilt of the sword. "I'll be fine," he told her.

"I'll stay with Callum and his father," she said. "I've nothing to fear from them. But Tom, be careful. Remember what Malvel said about Zepha."

Cold fear gripped Tom again. He didn't even know what Zepha was. How could he prepare to fight an Evil Beast when he had no idea what it looked like?

"Are you coming or not?" Lindon's harsh voice interrupted his thoughts.

"I'm coming," said Tom, pushing down his apprehension.

Elenna grasped his hand. "Good luck," she said.

Silver added an encouraging bark, and Storm whinnied.

"Don't worry. I'll be back soon," Tom promised.

He helped Lindon push the boat back into the water and scrambled over the side. Lindon raised the sail and soon the boat was scudding over the waves again. Tom looked back at the shore where Elenna, Silver and Storm stood. Already they seemed very small and distant.

The sky was covered with thick, grey cloud. As Lindon steered the boat out to sea, the wind grew even stronger. The water became choppy and the boat pitched up and down on the waves.

Tom gripped the side and stared down into the sea. He thought he could make out the movement of some dark shape far beneath the surface. Suddenly the water began to churn angrily and Tom gasped as he realised that the boat was swirling around in a huge circle. A whirlpool

was starting up – and he and Lindon were at the centre of it!

Lindon laughed. "Getting scared?" he taunted. "Do you want to change your mind?"

"No!" Tom was determined not to let Lindon see he was afraid. "This is what I've come for."

Lindon grunted and deftly steered the boat out of the whirlpool. Tom could tell he was a skilful sailor. Even so, the boat rocked dangerously and water slopped over the side, soaking Tom. Lindon guided the boat to the edge of the churning water. "I'll wait for you here," he said. "Mind you're not too long! Otherwise I'll be heading back to collect your horse."

Tom climbed onto the side of the boat. The water was circling faster than ever, opening up a cone-shaped passage into the depths of the sea. Tom's heart thumped in terror, but he knew he couldn't turn back. He remembered how he had dived into

the sea to meet Sepron, and had
emerged victorious.

"I have to do this," Tom muttered.
"For the Golden Armour. And to
defeat Malvel."

Tom took in a lungful of air, and
closed his mouth tightly. Then he
dived down into the sea.

7

INTO THE
WHIRLPOOL

At once the whirlpool sucked Tom
down into the depths of the ocean.
The force of the water dragged at
his clothes and wrenched his arms
and legs. Tom felt as if he were
being torn apart.

Swirling water was all around
him. Caught up in the powerful
current, Tom spun round and round.

He fought not to lose his bearings, but soon he couldn't tell whether he was facing the surface of the sea or down towards the ocean bed.

I'm going to drown! he thought frantically. Was this the end of his new Quest already?

Then pain stabbed through him as his flailing arm struck something hard. Instinctively he grabbed at it and found he was clinging to a spur of rock that thrust upwards from the ocean bed. Working his way along it, he managed to drag himself out of the force of the whirlpool and calm his panic.

Looking around, he saw the spires and hollows of a coral bed stretching into the distance. Then a

dull gleam of gold caught his eye.
On one spike of rock rested the
golden helmet.

Tom had never seen a helmet like it before. It was shaped like an eagle's head; the visor was moulded in the form of a hooked beak, and the golden surface was patterned to look like feathers.

Tom was amazed. He couldn't believe how easy this was! He would just collect the helmet, then swim back up to the boat.

Kicking away from the rock, Tom swam towards the golden gleam. But as he reached for the helmet, he spotted movement just beyond. A dark shadow was rising up from behind the rock. It was so huge that it took Tom a moment to realise it was a head, with staring, bulging eyes and a mouth like a

gaping beak. Seconds later the
body followed, with a mass of giant
tentacles. Tom could see through
the creature's skin, to where three
red hearts were pumping.

Zepha was a giant squid! More than that – a monster squid!

This was the Beast threatening the villagers with starvation by driving all the fish away. Panic froze Tom. How could he battle such a vast creature? Its eyes alone were as big as he was and the beak could swallow him up in one gulp.

Before Tom could make a dive for the helmet, the squid hurtled out of its shelter in the coral, its snaking tentacles reaching for Tom.

Tom felt his lungs start to hurt with the effort of holding his breath. As he pushed himself through the water, away from the grasping tentacles, he let a few precious bubbles of air escape from his mouth.

Now he was deep below the
surface with no air, and the
monster squid was between him
and the helmet.

What could he do now? And more

to the point: how was he going to get out of this alive?

8

UNEXPECTED HELP

Kicking out strongly, Tom tried
to swim for the surface while he
still had breath in his lungs. At
every moment he expected one of
Zepha's tentacles to fasten round
his ankles, dragging him back into
the depths.

Tom's head burst through the
surface of the sea; he coughed up
water and took in great gulps of

air. Blinking to clear his eyes, he spotted Lindon's boat rocking on the waves a few yards away, and swam carefully around the whirlpool towards it. When he reached the boat, Lindon leant over the side to help him on board.

"I reckoned I'd seen the last of you," said Lindon. There was a grudging respect in his tone of voice. He grasped Tom's hand and shook it firmly.

"I reckon you can keep your horse after that." He looked at Tom curiously. "What did you see down there?"

"You have to take me back!" Tom gasped. "I need to pick up Elenna."

Lindon saw the determination

in his face and nodded. Quickly he hauled on the ropes and soon the boat was plunging back towards the beach.

Elenna was waiting for Tom at the water's edge, holding his sword and shield. She flung them down and hugged Tom as he leapt ashore. Silver bounded around him excitedly, letting out a howl of welcome.

"You're safe!" Elenna exclaimed. "But where's the helmet?"

"At the bottom of the sea," Tom replied. "Guarded by a giant squid."

"Zepha is a squid?"

"Yes. Elenna – he's huge. A monster." Hesitatingly he added, "I'm not sure I can defeat him."

"Yes, you can." Elenna's voice was encouraging. "Or we can do it together."

Tom was warmed by his friend's courage and loyalty. "I was hoping you'd say that," he said.

He turned back to Lindon, to see the fisherman already heading away, towards the people still huddled around the fire. He was carrying the basket of fish he had caught earlier.

"Hey!" Tom called out. "I need you to take me out there again."

"I've had my share of risk for today," Lindon said. He shook his head regretfully. "I'm not going back out again. Sorry." He strode off towards the fire.

Elenna and Tom looked at each

other. They both knew that Elenna was skilful at handling a boat.

"Do you think we should take it?" Elenna whispered.

"We had to do that last time, when we freed Sepron the Sea Serpent," Tom replied. "It's for the good of the people here. We have no choice."

When they were sure that no one was looking, Tom fastened on his scabbard and put his shield into the boat. Then he and Elenna climbed in. Silver watched them, letting out a mournful whine.

"All right, you can come, too," said Elenna. The wolf's ears went up and he took a flying leap into the boat, which rocked from side to side.

"Storm will be fine," Elenna added.

"Callum is looking after him."

Tom's fear returned as Elenna guided the boat out to sea. He imagined one of Zepha's giant tentacles lashing out of the water and pulling the boat down into the depths. All three of them would drown.

"Are you ready for this? It's very dangerous…" he began. Had he made a mistake coming back for his friend?

"We wanted to come, didn't we, Silver?" Elenna said calmly.

Silver gave a yelp of agreement.

"But you haven't seen Zepha. He's terrifying."

Tom almost asked Elenna to turn

back. But then he saw a blue glow forming in the air just ahead of the boat. Inside it, Aduro appeared. Tom could still see the tossing waves through his robes. The wizard had sent an illusion of himself, just as he had many times before.

"Don't give up hope, Tom," he said with a smile. "Have you forgotten the help you have with you?"

"What do you mean?" Tom asked.

"When you freed Sepron you were given one of his teeth, which you fixed into your shield," Aduro reminded him.

"Of course!" Tom *had* forgotten.

Aduro went on. "If you rub the tooth, Sepron himself will come to help. But remember: as a Good Beast of Avantia, he can only attack Zepha in order to protect you." The wizard's form began to fade. "Good luck!" he called out before he disappeared altogether.

Tom grabbed his shield and polished Sepron's tooth hard with the sleeve of his tunic.

At first nothing happened. Could Wizard Aduro have been wrong? Or was Sepron so far away that he couldn't feel the summons?

As they sailed further out to sea, Elenna leant over the side. "I can see something moving!" she cried.

Tom's stomach lurched. *Sepron?* he asked himself. *Or Zepha?*

Joy flooded through him as a huge head and arching neck burst out of

the sea, glittering streams of water
pouring from it. Tom gazed up at
Sepron's shining eyes and green
scales.

"It worked!" Elenna laughed.

The great sea serpent arched his
neck protectively over the boat.
Then he dived beneath the waves
again. Even though Tom couldn't
see him, he knew that the Beast

was there, ready to help and protect them. Would it be enough? Or was Malvel's Evil Beast too strong even for Sepron?

By now Tom could see the turbulent water at the edge of the whirlpool. Silver began to whine and pace back and forth along the boards of the boat.

"He knows something's wrong," Elenna said grimly.

Gripping his shield, Tom climbed onto the boat's side, Elenna scrambling up beside him.

"I'll distract Zepha," Tom said. "When he comes after me, you grab the helmet and swim back to the boat as fast as you can."

Elenna nodded.

Tom gazed down into the whirlpool. Just below the surface Sepron was circling, waiting.

"Stay, Silver," Elenna told the wolf. He whimpered a little, but settled down obediently in the bottom of the boat with his nose on his paws.

"This is it," Tom said.

Together, he and Elenna dived into the whirlpool.

THE ANGER OF ZEPHA

This time the weight of Tom's sword and shield took him down faster. He managed to keep his sense of direction, swimming in a spiral down to the sea bed. He looked up. Above him, Elenna swam with Sepron.

Soon Tom spotted the coral reef and the golden glint of the helmet.

He pointed Elenna towards it. Elenna put her thumbs up and began to head in that direction.

Then the huge form of Zepha came into view behind the spires of coral. Tom saw Elenna's mouth open in a cry of horror. Valuable air bubbled away to the surface. Tom had to help! He swam close to her and gripped her shoulder encouragingly.

Then they swam on together towards the menacing shape of the monster squid.

As they drew closer, Tom could see the giant tentacles waving gently in the underwater tide. Zepha was curled up as if he were resting. But Tom wasn't fooled.

In a sudden movement, Elenna darted towards the helmet. Tom swam nearer, despite the danger, hoping to distract the Evil Beast. But he got too close. As Tom turned to swim away, hoping Zepha would be lured to follow, a tentacle lashed out and wrapped itself round his ankle.

Tom tugged furiously, trying to free himself. He spotted Elenna swimming towards him, but waved her back, towards the helmet.

He could feel the tentacle tightening. It was cutting off his blood supply; his foot was growing numb. He kicked out, trying to swim for the surface, but the tentacle held him back. Starting to

panic, Tom gulped in a mouthful
of sea water and began to choke.
Then he caught another glimpse of
Elenna. Her knife in her hand, she
was swimming down towards the
giant squid. She pulled her arm
back, and the knife flashed in a
shaft of sunlight that pierced the

sea-green gloom. Then she thrust the blade deep into the tough muscle of Zepha's tentacle.

The Beast's pale eyes opened wide in a spasm of pain and fury. Tom felt the grip on his ankle loosen. Drawing his sword, he slashed angrily at the tentacle. Red blood

billowed out into the water. The tip of the tentacle fell away as the Beast thrashed wildly in agony. Tom was free – for the moment.

He swam away from Zepha, but the squid heaved his injured body up from the coral bed and gave chase, closing the gap between himself and Tom with frightening speed.

Then Tom saw Sepron swimming towards them. His scales glittered and his eyes flashed with fury. The sea serpent's jaws gaped as he snapped angrily at Zepha. His teeth punctured the squid's leathery skin and gripped tightly.

Zepha twisted with rage and pain, and squirted a huge cloud

of black ink from the underside of
his body into the sea serpent's face.
Sepron reared back, blinded by the
ink, and thrashed his head from side
to side as the black cloud spread.
His grip on Zepha loosened as he
rolled over and over in the water,
trying to clear his sight.

Free again, the monster squid
shot after Tom. His tentacles
whipped through the sea, churning
up underwater currents. Tom was
battered around by the angry water.
Where was Elenna? He couldn't
see her! He swiped at Zepha with
his sword, aiming at the three hearts
that pulsed beneath the squid's skin.

But one flailing tentacle knocked
the sword out of his hand. Tom

stared in horror as it sank and was lost in the darkness of the green, watery depths.

Tom had never felt so alone. Sepron couldn't help him, and Elenna had vanished. His arms and legs ached with exhaustion, and the air in his lungs was running out again. He struck out for the surface, but he knew he would never swim fast enough to escape, and he had no weapon left with which to fight.

Zepha swam towards Tom, his mouth open wide. His pale eyes gleamed. One of his tentacles coiled round Tom's waist. Terrified, Tom felt himself being dragged closer to that gaping hole. He held up his

shield as a last attempt to defend
himself. But Zepha's mouth was
big enough to engulf the shield and

Tom as well.

There was nothing more Tom could do. Malvel had won.

10

VICTORY?

Suddenly the water swirled as Elenna swam in front of Tom, his sword gripped in one hand, her knife in the other. Fearlessly she plunged down and forced the sword into Zepha's open mouth, jamming the beak open. The squid's bulging eyes flared with anger. He released his grip on Tom and flung all his tentacles at Elenna. More bubbles escaped from her mouth as she gasped in alarm. She turned and swam rapidly away.

Tom knew he hadn't much time. The sword wouldn't keep Zepha back for long and he couldn't hold his breath for much longer. He had to find the helmet, but in the battle with the squid he had lost his sense of direction. He peered down through the gloom, but he couldn't see the telltale glint of gold.

To his relief, Sepron came gliding through the greenish darkness. Tom could tell he had recovered his sight; his eyes glared with anger and he was heading straight for Zepha. He swooped down and wrapped his green coils around the squid. He twisted to and fro so that Zepha couldn't squirt ink into his face again, or grip him with his tentacles.

Sepron clutched the giant squid tighter and tighter with his coils. Tom could hardly believe what he was seeing. It looked as if the sea serpent was squeezing the life out of Zepha. Astonished, Tom watched as the edges of Zepha started to blur. He looked round for Elenna, who had reappeared, and pointed frantically. Something was happening! Rippling movements came from beneath Zepha's skin as the Evil Beast writhed in agony.

Suddenly the monster squid's three pulsing, red hearts shattered into tiny glinting pieces, too many

for Tom to count, and his skin burst
open, tearing cruelly. Tom struggled
not to gasp underwater as thousands
of tiny squid shot out, swimming as
if they feared for their lives. Zepha's
empty, papery skin began to sink
slowly down into the gloom, towards
the sea bed. He was no more.

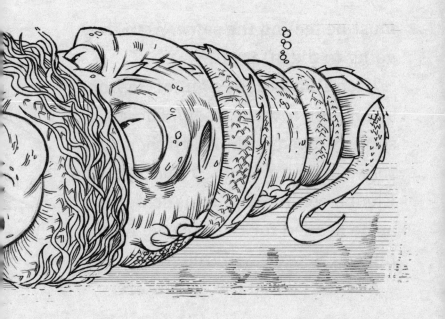

Elenna grabbed Tom's sword before it could fall out of sight once again. Tom swam after her, gazing round for a glimpse of the helmet. Then he spotted its golden gleam.

But exhaustion made his limbs heavy. He had no air left. His lungs were screaming with pain. Elenna must be feeling the same. Were they going to die after all?

Then Tom caught sight of Sepron swimming towards them. The sea serpent dived underneath them and rose slowly upwards so that Tom and Elenna could cling to his scaly neck as he headed for the surface. Tom hugged Sepron with relief.

As they passed the coral spire

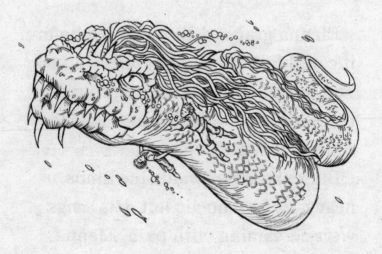

where the golden helmet rested, Tom reached out and grasped it by the hooked beak.

Sepron's neck rose out of the water just beside the boat. Tom and Elenna clung on for a moment more, gasping air into their tortured lungs. Silver sprang up and rested his front paws on the side of the boat, letting out an astonished yelp.

Then the sea serpent lowered his neck. Tom and Elenna gently rolled off into the bottom of the boat. Silver pushed up close to Elenna, nosing her. She rolled onto her back and allowed the wolf to lick her face. Her chest rose and fell as she gasped for air. Then she reached out a hand to ruffle Silver's fur. She was all right.

"Thank you, Sepron,"Tom panted, reaching up to pat the serpent's gleaming scales. "We couldn't have done it without you."

Sepron bowed his head and gave each of them a friendly touch with his nose before sinking back beneath the waves again. Tom caught a last glimpse of his green coils as he swam away into the open sea. He felt warmed by the thought that the Beast who had once been his foe had saved their lives.

"Well," he said with an exhausted sigh. "We've got the helmet."

"Why don't you try it on?" Elenna asked, climbing to her feet.

Tom hesitated for a moment, turning the helmet over between his hands. The gold shone brightly and he could see how skilfully the helmet was crafted from the time he had spent working in his uncle's forge.

Could it really be for him? Was he worthy of wearing the helmet that once belonged to the Master of the Beasts of Avantia?

"Go on!" Elenna urged him.

Tom raised the helmet and put it on his head. Instantly he felt it shrink to fit him. He gasped. His eyesight had suddenly grown stronger! He could see the people on the shoreline; Callum's father was mending a fishing net and Lindon was squatting by the fire, drinking something from a bowl. Further away from the sea, Callum was leading Storm along the edge of the trees. Tom could even see the whites of the stallion's eyes as he paced up and down.

"This is amazing," he exclaimed. "I can see everything! I just wish my father, Taladon, could see me."

"He'd be so proud of you," Elenna told him.

Tom and Elenna hugged each other.

Triumph bubbled up inside Tom. The first part of his new Quest was over! He had retrieved the helmet. And now he was determined that it wouldn't be long before he found the other five parts of the armour, too.

"We've only just started," he said to Elenna. "I'm not giving up until I have every piece of the Golden Armour."

Elenna smiled in agreement. "Let's get back to shore," she said gently.

She pulled up the sail and began to guide the boat towards the beach.

They were halfway back when a familiar blue glow began to appear before them, and Aduro seemed to stand on the waves.

But this time he was not alone.

Standing behind him was Malvel, who held a slim, jewelled dagger to the wizard's neck. Aduro's face was set hard, as if he was refusing to show fear.

Tom couldn't understand what he was seeing. "Get away from him!" he shouted at Malvel.

The Dark Wizard smiled. "So you have the golden helmet," he sneered. "But I don't suppose you feel quite so pleased with yourself now, do you?"

"I don't believe this!" Tom cried. "It's just an illusion. You could never take Aduro prisoner. You haven't the power."

"I'm afraid I do." Malvel dug the point of the dagger into Aduro's neck. "Tell them, fool."

"This is a true vision," Wizard Aduro said reluctantly. "Perhaps I was foolish, and didn't guard myself well enough. I am Malvel's prisoner."

"I'll free you!" Tom said defiantly.

Malvel's cruel laughter sounded. "You can try."

Tom reached out to Aduro, but his hand passed through air. "Tell me what to do!"

"You can free me," Wizard Aduro said. "But first you must find the full suit of armour... It is the only way."

"That will never happen," Malvel interrupted, the dagger digging into the Good Wizard's neck. "You'll fail the next test, Tom, when you have to face my second Evil Beast – Claw."

"We'll do it," Tom vowed. "We'll free Aduro and destroy you once and for all."

"I can hold out against him," Aduro insisted, though his face was pale. "But you must complete the Quest!"

Malvel's laughter rang out again as the vision faded.

Tom and Elenna exchanged a horrified glance. All Tom's sense of triumph had vanished. He could only think about Aduro in the clutches of Malvel.

As they beached the boat, Callum came up to them, leading Storm. Tom had been wondering how to explain to Lindon why they had taken his boat without permission, but thankfully, the fisherman was

nowhere in sight. Tom climbed out of
the boat and took the stallion's reins,
stroking his nose.

"Thanks," he said to Callum.
Glancing out to sea again, he added,
"I don't think you'll have any more
trouble."

Callum met his gaze steadily. "I
won't ask questions," he said. "You
saved us once before, and that's
good enough for me." He bent to
give Silver a pat. "You're welcome to
come and stay with my family if you
want."

"Thank you, but we can't," Tom
said regretfully. "We have other
duties."

"I understand," said Callum. "But I
hope you'll come back when you can.

You'll always find friends here."

Taking up his sword and shield, Tom climbed into Storm's saddle with Elenna behind him.

"Farewell!" Elenna called.

"Farewell, and good luck!" Callum replied.

With a last wave, Tom and Elenna headed up the beach to find the road that led back inland.

Tom felt as if a huge weight was pressing upon him. "This is our most important Quest yet," he said.

"I know." Elenna tightened her arms around his waist. "This time we've got to succeed."

Tom nodded. She was right. The Quest wasn't about his need to prove himself, not any more. It wasn't even about the magical Golden Armour.

It was about rescuing Aduro.

Could they do it?

"While there's blood in my veins," Tom swore, "I'll never give up!"

CONGRATULATIONS, YOU HAVE COMPLETED THIS QUEST!

At the end of each chapter you were awarded a special gold coin.
The QUEST in this book was worth an amazing 11 coins.

Look at the Beast Quest totem picture inside the back cover of this book to see how far you've come in your journey to become

MASTER OF THE BEASTS.

The more books you read, the more coins you will collect!

Do you want your own
Beast Quest Totem?

1. Cut out and collect the coin below
2. Go to the Beast Quest website
3. Download and print out your totem
4. Add your coin to the totem
www.beastquest.co.uk/totem

Don't miss the next exciting Beast Quest book, CLAW THE GIANT MONKEY!

Read on for a sneak peek...

CHAPTER ONE

CROSSING THE WINDING RIVER

Tom guided his black stallion Storm inland, away from Avantia's western shore. Elenna sat behind him, her arms around his waist.

Silver, Elenna's pet wolf, padded quietly alongside. Struggling with Zepha the Monster Squid had been their toughest challenge yet. If it hadn't been for Sepron, the great sea serpent and protector of Avantia's waters, they might never have defeated the Evil Beast.

Stored safely in Storm's saddlebag lay a magnificent golden helmet, shaped like the head of an eagle. It was the first piece from the great suit of Golden Armour, which gave magical powers to its rightful owner. The armour had belonged to the Master of the Beasts and had been destined to pass to Tom as a reward for completing his first Quest. Now it was Tom's fate to recover the six pieces, which had been stolen by the Dark Wizard Malvel and scattered across Avantia. But Malvel had charged six Evil Beasts with protecting each piece. Zepha had been the first, with the helmet as the prize. There were five more Beasts to overcome and five pieces of armour to collect.

But that was not all. For Malvel had taken more than the armour. He had kidnapped Aduro, King Hugo's wizard and Tom and Elenna's friend and protector.

"I'm worried about Aduro," Elenna said now.

"That's why we have to find and defeat this next Beast, Claw, whatever he is," said Tom. "We will soon find all six pieces of the armour and, when our Quest is complete, we will rescue Aduro. As he told us himself, there's no other way!"

Silver yapped in excitement, and Storm tossed his fine head.

"Malvel may have Aduro," said Tom," but we still have Aduro's enchanted map. Let's see if it will tell us where we can find Claw."

Read
CLAW THE GIANT MONKEY
to find out more!

FIGHT THE BEASTS,
FEAR THE MAGIC

Are you a BEAST QUEST mega fan?
Do you want to know about all the latest news,
competitions and books before anyone else?

Then join our Quest Club!

Visit the BEAST QUEST website
and sign up today!

www.beastquest.co.uk

Discover the new Beast Quest mobile game from

Available free on iOS and Android

 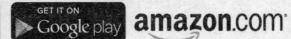

Guide Tom on his Quest to free the Good Beasts
of Avantia from Malvel's evil spells.

Battle the Beasts, defeat the minions,
unearth the secrets and collect
rewards as you journey through the
Kingdom of Avantia.

DOWNLOAD THE APP TO BEGIN
THE ADVENTURE NOW!